Dedicated to the truly magical Team Bodhi,
who have held my hand on the most difficult path,
and to our little warrior himself. HPx


To my son Elias, for being my inspiration.
And to my husband, for believing in me
more than I do. HTx

ISBN 978-1-78270-549-9

Text copyright © Hannah Peckham
Artwork copyright © Award Publications Limited

First published 2023

Published by Award Publications Limited,
The Old Riding School, Welbeck,
Worksop, S80 3LR

 /awardpublications   @award.books   @award_books
www.awardpublications.co.uk

23-1062 1

Printed in China

# BRONTY'S BATTLE CRY

## Hannah Peckham
### Illustrated by Hanna Tkachenko

award

In a far-away land where
swamps gurgle and bubble,
squabbles break out
at the first sign of trouble.
And all dinosaurs,
horned, armoured or spiny,
have to be fearsome,
no matter how tiny.

It is here where the tribes meet,
like each year before,
to show off their braveness
by how loud they can roar.

Where they bellow their battle cries,
a deafening chorus,
that is all except
for one young brontosaurus.

Yes, Bronty was different,
his eyesight was blurred.
His hearing was how
he kept up with the herd.

Getting lost was a problem
when home was not near,
or tripping on tree roots
that just seemed to appear.

Loud noise was confusing,
the herd could be frightening,

like the rumbles and bangs
of thunder and lightning.

And the need to be brave,
whatever the struggle,
even when feelings
were all of a muddle.

Yet he heard the beauty that they never saw,
as they bickered about who'd got the best roar.
You see, Bronty was special, for he loved lullabies.
His voice sang in harmonies, not battle cries.

Miss Raptor despaired
when she heard Bronty's song,
"My dear brontosaurus,
you've got it all wrong.

ROAARR

"A song will not stop you
from being the prey.
You need to be ROARSOME
to scare them away."

When the herd teased him,
as often they would,
and spoke of his *couldn'ts*
and not of his *coulds*,
he'd retreat, on his own,
back into his cave,
safe and secure,
no need to be brave.

And there in the quiet he heard beautiful things,
like the delicate flutter of ladybird wings.
He'd hear whispered secrets that came on sea breezes,
and beetles with tickles that turned into sneezes.

The falling of conkers from trees blown and shaken.
A dormant volcano soon to awaken.
Just a hint of a murmur of the wind's distant song,
and Bronty would find himself humming along.

And this little knowing
helped him hold tight,
as he tried to fit in
and learn how to fight.
Until the day came
when the tribes got together,
the way it had been
for almost... forever!

Here they all gathered
from the land and the sky,
ready to hear Bronty's
first battle cry!
T-Rex went first;
a frightening fellow,
with an utterly fearsome,
ground-shaking bellow.

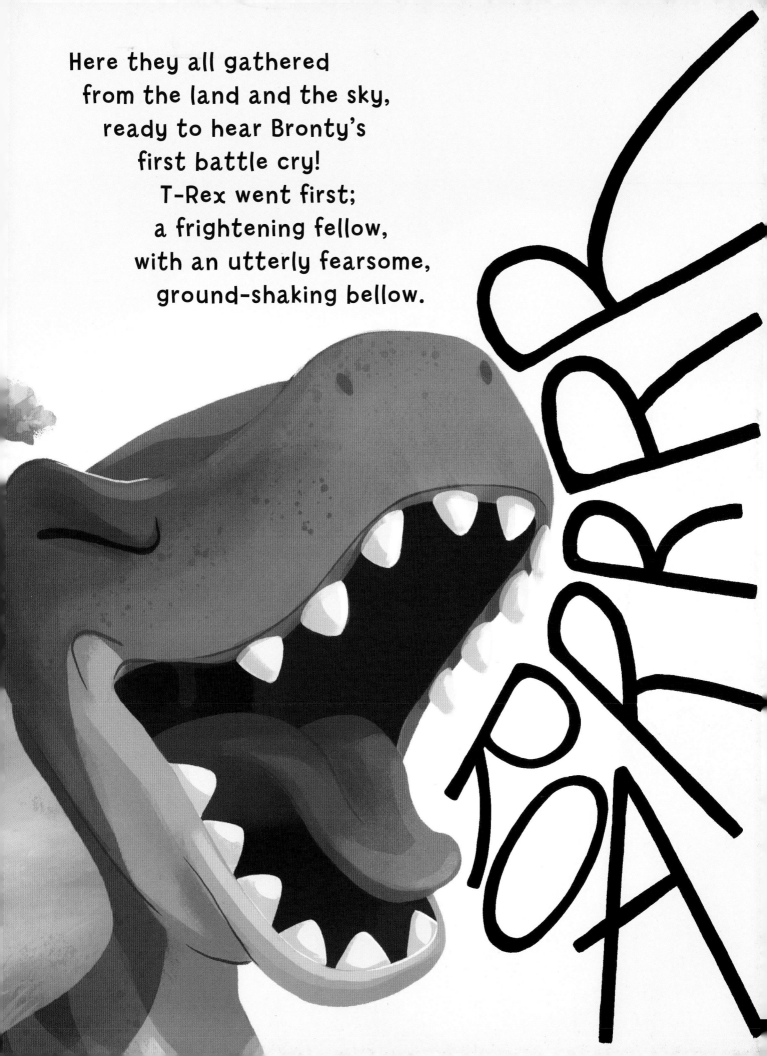

RRRRRRR
ROAR

Diplodocus was next with a proud battle chant,
whilst Bronty was thinking 'I simply just can't!'

Even the tiny microraptor did well,

but when Bronty went up,
he tripped and he fell.

As he lay in the dirt,
confused and blinking,
he couldn't believe it -
he could *hear* what they were thinking!

MY ORN IS OLITTLE!

MY ARMS ARE too SMALL!

I WISH I WAS FASTER!

I WISH I WAS TALL!

The longer he listened,
the more he realised,
they didn't believe
in their own battle cries.

Each dino was worried,
a little like him,
that if they didn't roar
then they wouldn't fit in.

You see, ranting and raving
can hide frightened hearts.
Fear is often the reason
why shouting can start.
Faking you're brave
to maintain your pride
won't stop you from feeling
your feelings inside.

So, with a deep breath, Bronty sang of his fear,

which actually helped make it all disappear.

He sung of his strengths and the beauty he knew,

and as he did this, his braveness,

# it grew!

Bronty turned to the others and he sang to them too,
about all of their talents and all they could do!
He said, "Frightening others won't help you at all,
when outside is tough but inside feels small."

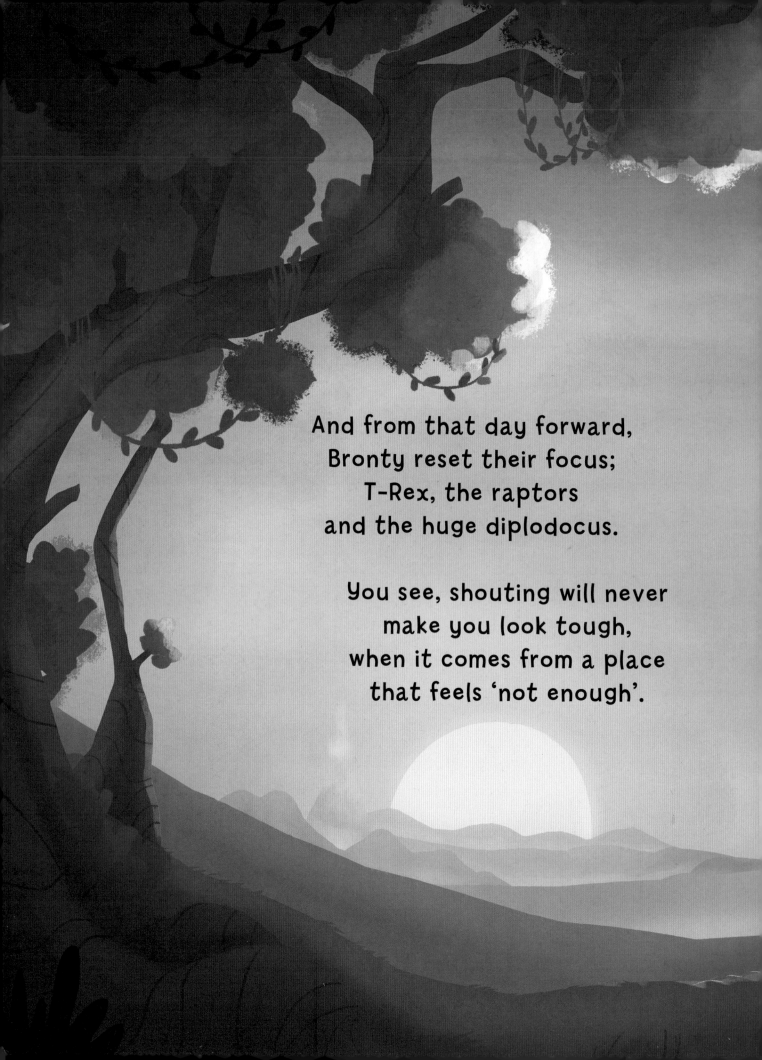

And from that day forward,
Bronty reset their focus;
T-Rex, the raptors
and the huge diplodocus.

You see, shouting will never
make you look tough,
when it comes from a place
that feels 'not enough'.

So, sing of your talents
and of others' too.
There's nothing to fear,
being perfectly you!
Yes, belt out your story;
it's the best one to sing.
If you can do that,
you can do anything!

# Activities

## Positive self-talk

Think of your thoughts as being like flowers.

The ones that you feed and water will grow the best.

If you only feed and water the negative thoughts, those are the ones that will grow bigger.

But, if you feed and water the positive ones, you will have a head FULL of happy and wonderful thoughts, like a garden full of beautiful flowers!

Why not try drawing a flower (like Bronty is here), and on each petal write something good about yourself.

I HEAR BEAUTY

I CAN SiNG!

I AM KIND

By remembering these positive things about yourself, you are watering the positive flowers and helping them to grow big and strong! Put your flower somewhere you can see it every day - perhaps by your bed or where you have breakfast!

# Share the love

Did you know, SMILES are catching? Science suggests that when you see someone smiling, you feel amazing and want to smile too! We also know that being kind to others makes us feel good about ourselves as well!

Why not set yourself a challenge to do, or say, something nice to someone every day this week? You could plan it on a chart, like Bronty and his friends have done here.

# What's your battle cry?

When Bronty sang of his fear, it helped to make it disappear. Singing positive thoughts helped him to feel brave. What helps you when you feel worried?

Have a go at creating your own battle cry, listing all the things you love about yourself! You could even make it into a picture! If you are stuck, why not try using Bronty's helpful guide below.

I am good at...

I can...

I am loved by...

I am brave because...

I am proud of myself because...

I am perfectly me!

I am unstoppable when...

Photograph by Lotty Staples for #pantstoleukaemia campaign

Hannah Peckham is a counsellor, children's author and mother of a beloved son, Bodhi. During the creation of this book, their world was turned on its head when Bodhi was diagnosed with acute lymphoblastic leukaemia.

Devastated but determined, Hannah is now on a mission to raise awareness and funds to find a kinder cure for this life-threatening illness. Which is why 25p will be donated to Leukaemia UK for every copy of this book sold in the UK, and why Bodhi's **#pantstoleukaemia** campaign is helping to fund research to improve and save more lives.

So, thank you for buying this book and supporting this vital work. If you'd like to know more, follow **@h.j.peckham** on Instagram or visit **www.leukaemiauk.org.uk**

Registered charity no. 1154856